Bantam Books in the Choose Your Own Adventure® Series
Ask your bookseller for the books you have missed

Choose Your Own Adventure Books for younger readers

SABOTAGE

BY JAY LEIBOLD

ILLUSTRATED BY RALPH REESE

A Packard/Montgomery Book

BANTAM BOOKS
TORONTO · NEW YORK · LONDON · SYDNEY · AUCKLAND

RL 4, IL age 10 and up

SABOTAGE

A Bantam Book / November 1984

CHOOSE YOUR OWN ADVENTURE® is a registered trademark of
Bantam Books, Inc. Registered in U.S. Patent and Trademark
Office and elsewhere.

Original conception of Edward Packard

Produced by Cloverdale Press Inc.,
133 Fifth Avenue, New York, NY 10003.

ISBN 0-553-24525-2

Published simultaneously in the United States and Canada

PRINTED IN THE UNITED STATES OF AMERICA

O   0 9 8 7 6 5 4 3 2 1

For Shannon and Ray

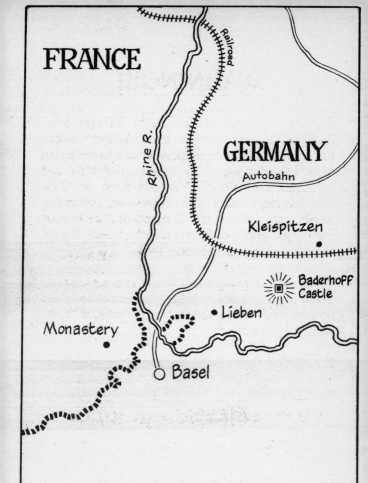

WARNING!!!

Do not read this book straight through from beginning to end. There are many different adventures you can have as a World War II secret agent trying to rescue your friends from a Nazi prison cell in Baderhoff Castle. As you read along, you'll be able to make choices. Your choices will determine whether you outwit the Gestapo and save your friends, or meet a chilling end at the hands of your archenemy Herr Kruptsch.

There are many ways to succeed in your mission. You are responsible because *you* choose. After you make a choice, follow the instructions to see what happens next.

Be careful! Spies lie in wait for you, and traps abound. People are not always what they seem to be. Good luck.

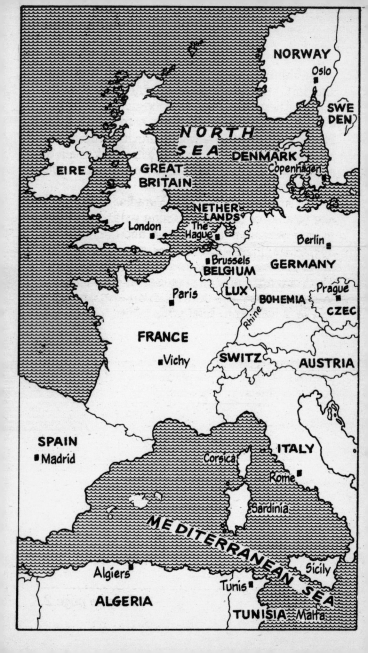

Casablanca, 1942: You make your way through the dark, narrow streets of the city to the Paradise Club. There you are to rendezvous with two French Resistance fighters for a mission for the Secret Forces. You take a roundabout route because Casablanca is crawling with spies. Even as you stepped off the plane, you could sense eyes following you.

The smoky lounge of the Paradise is filled with the sounds of spinning roulette wheels, German soldiers singing patriotic songs, and the babble of many languages. You spot your two Resistance contacts: Simone in her red beret, and Raoul with his drooping mustache. You greet them with a nod and follow them to a back room where Colonel de Grelle is waiting to brief you.

Turn to page 2.

You settle into a worn leather chair. A map of Europe is on the wall behind de Grelle. Your mission: to penetrate German lines, make your way through Occupied France to the Baderhoff Castle high in the Bavarian Alps, and rescue two Resistance fighters held there—the legendary brother-and-sister team of Jean-Paul and Marie LaRoche.

"I'm sure I don't need to remind you of the importance of these two," de Grelle says, casting a

glance at you. No, he does not need to remind you. They are two of your dearest friends. Together you have completed many missions in the Middle East and the south of France.

"Time is short," continues de Grelle. "Soon they will break down under interrogation and reveal the names and locations of all our people in southern France. No one can resist the Gestapo." He shakes his head. "They are fiends."

Turn to page 5.

"We don't have any time to waste," you say. "Let's parachute in. Raoul, can you show us where to drop?"

"Yes," he says reluctantly. He unfolds the map and points to a mountain slope near the castle. "That's the best place. It's hidden from the Germans but only a couple of days' ski from the castle."

Soon the three of you are 3,000 feet above the snowcapped peaks of the Bavarian Alps. You put your cross-country skis and mountain-climbing equipment into your packs, shrug them onto your shoulders, and clip into your parachute harnesses. As the plane swoops low and you line up to jump, Raoul's face goes completely white. He clings to the door of the plane.

"Wait a minute," Simone says to him. "I've got an idea. First, close your eyes. Now, relax your muscles and imagine a soft bed of down." Her voice is soothing, and Raoul obeys. But no sooner does he begin to relax than she gives him a good shove out the door. You leap out after him. For a few seconds you free-fall; then you pull the ripcord and float down into German territory.

Turn to page 12.

You agree to meet Raoul and Simone at the Café Paris the next morning. As you leave the briefing room, de Grelle pulls you aside and hands you a sealed envelope. "This is for your eyes only. Open it once you have reached the castle—and not before," he murmurs. "One more thing: Our agents have spotted Herr Kruptsch in Casablanca."

Kruptsch! You can hardly believe your ears. The cruel SS agent is your archenemy from previous missions in Beirut, Cairo, and Lyons. The stakes must be pretty high for the German Command to have sent Kruptsch.

"Good luck, my friend," de Grelle says, shaking your hand. "I know how much Jean-Paul and Marie mean to you."

You step out the back door of the Paradise into the foggy Casablanca night. Immediately you sense someone waiting in the shadows. You move quickly through the alleys, occasionally catching a glimpse of a figure following you. It appears to be a man with a hat pulled down over his eyes. You make a few evasive moves, but still he follows you. He's starting to make you nervous.

If you turn and confront your pursuer, turn to page 11.

If you try to give him the slip, turn to page 18.

You turn to Raoul. "Where can we find a steamer with a crew that shares our sympathies?"

"Follow me," says Raoul, and he leads you down to the docks, to a boat named the *Mermaid*. It looks old and beat-up, which is just what you want. After some haggling with the captain, you come to terms. You, Simone, and Raoul put on ragged black pants, baggy wool sweaters, and fishermen's caps. The captain starts up the engine, and you chug out into the rolling blue Mediterranean.

The hull groans and creaks as the steamer heads toward the French coast. The smell of rotting fish and the tossing of the waves make you feel a little sick. You wonder if this leaky old tub can really make it all the way across the sea.

On the morning of the second day the captain points to a shape on the horizon. "Take a look," he says, handing you the binoculars.

It is a German patrol boat.

Go on to the next page.

"There's no way we can outrun it," you say. "We'll just have to wait for it to pull up."

You wait nervously. If the German captain demands to come aboard and finds your equipment for the mission, you're done for. You can try to bluff and hope he believes your story. Or you can attack the German boat, hoping the element of surprise will help you overcome its firepower.

If you choose to fight, turn to page 21.

If you choose to bluff, turn to page 32.

The next morning you meet Simone and Raoul at the Café Paris, and the three of you pore over maps of the Mediterranean region. Raoul knows the castle and the surrounding area. Simone is a genius with explosives and a top-flight mountaineer. Both of them speak flawless German, which is just as well because your knowledge of the language is limited.

Simone ticks off a checklist of equipment: "Thirty pounds of high-grade dynamite. Twenty time-delay fuses. Food and winter clothing. Three German officers' uniforms, and three sets of forged transit papers."

"Good," you say. "Now we have to decide how to get to the castle."

"The way I see it," says Raoul, "our best bet is to disguise ourselves as fishermen, hire a tramp steamer, and sail to the French coast. From there we can go overland through France to the castle."

"But there's another choice," Simone breaks in. "Hitch a ride with one of our reconnaissance planes and parachute into the Alps behind German lines."

"That's too risky," Raoul protests. "Besides, I'm scared of heights."

"It's risky, yes, but also much quicker," Simone replies.

They look to you to break the deadlock.

If you agree with Simone, turn to page 4.

If you prefer Raoul's plan, turn to page 6.

The avalanche moves at a terrifying speed. You struggle to get onto your back and swim on the cascade.

When your frightening slide finally comes to an end, you find that you are buried in only a couple of feet of snow. Somehow you managed to stay on top of the avalanche. You dig yourself out, then call, "Simone! Raoul!"

"Here I am!"

It's Simone!

"We were lucky," she says when she climbs up to your side. "We were on the edge of the avalanche. But not Raoul. I found him down there. He never had a chance."

You must decide what to do after this disaster. You and Simone are frozen, exhausted, and bruised all over. Common sense tells you to stop and make camp for the night. But that might give the Alpencorps a chance to catch up to you.

If you choose to go on, turn to page 13.

If you decide to make camp, turn to page 15.

You bind and gag the protesting Raoul and lock him in an unoccupied bathroom.

"If you're telling the truth and Marie and Jean-Paul aren't here, we'll be back to get you," says Simone.

"And if you're lying," you say, "well—your friends will find you soon enough." Then the two of you set off to find Marie and Jean-Paul.

"We have a problem," says Simone as you lead her down a corridor. "If we can't trust Raoul, we can't trust the map he drew for us."

"Exactly," you say. "And that's why we're going to the opposite wing of the castle."

Turn to page 81.

"Who are you and what do you want?" you shout at the man who's been following you.

He steps out into the light. His face reminds you of a squirrel's. His hands are buried deep in the pockets of his trench coat.

"Put your hands where I can see them," you say.

He spreads his hands before him. "I j-just wanted to tell you something," he stutters nervously. His eyes dart about. "I have . . . i-information for you."

"What kind of information?"

"V-very important information. About your mission."

"What mission?"

"You know—to r-rescue your friends." He steps closer and whispers, "But I cannot t-tell you here. Kruptsch's agents are everywhere. We must g-go someplace secret."

You are in a quandary. If he has information about Kruptsch, it may be important to listen to what he has to say. But can you trust him?

If you agree to go with him, turn to page 23.

If you refuse, turn to page 80.

The snow cushions your landing and you find Raoul and Simone nearby. Raoul is pleased that he made a successful jump. You bury your chutes and put on your skis. Suddenly a wisp of snow rises from the ground behind Simone. A split second later you hear the rifle report. You look down the mountain and see the crack alpine soldiers of the German Army.

"The Alpencorps!" you exclaim. "How could they have found us so soon?"

Turn to page 16.

Covering your tracks as best you can, you and Simone press on. After several hours you come across an old shepherd's hut at the bottom of a gully.

"We've got to hole up somewhere to rest and recover from our bruises," you say. "This looks like a good place."

"Phew!" says Simone as she stoops to enter the place. "It smells as if the sheep lived here along with the shepherd."

"I'm sure they did," you say with a laugh. "Anyway, the smell won't hurt us."

As it turns out, the smell *helps* you. Sometime later the two of you are jolted from an exhausted sleep by the sound of dogs barking and men calling in German. The Alpencorps! Two of them are quite close.

"This is a fool's errand," complains one soldier.

"But we found only one body," replies another.

"It's obvious the other two were buried by the avalanche," says the first. "There weren't any tracks leading away from the area."

"Then why did the dogs lead us here?" asks the second.

"There's an old shepherd's hut below; they smell the sheep," says the first. "Remember, these dogs were bred to herd the flocks. It's been in their blood for generations."

The men call off the dogs, and their voices fade. At last you're sure the Alpencorps is gone.

Turn to page 65.

You draw to within three feet of your friends. Suddenly you push a passing businessman into the back of one of the Gestapo guards. He turns and starts to argue with the businessman, who turns to point the finger at you. But you and Simone have already circled around in front of Jean-Paul and Marie. Simone knocks down the other Gestapo agent, and Marie and Jean-Paul make a dash for freedom—with you and Simone right behind.

It doesn't take long for the Gestapo men to realize what has happened. They start to chase you, but with your head start you manage to lose them in the crowd. You run out of the station and jump on a bus.

A couple of miles down the road, the four of you get off. Jean-Paul and Marie both give you a hug. "How did you find out we were taken to Munich?" Jean-Paul asks.

"It was a lucky guess," you say with a smile.

You'll have to be very cautious in getting your friends back to France, but with your false papers and uniforms you're confident you can do it.

The End

You and Simone dig trenches in the snow for your sleeping bags, then crawl inside them. Despite the cold and wet, you are soon fast asleep.

You are jolted awake by the barking of dogs. Dogs? You sit bolt upright. Ten meters away is an Alpencorps captain. His rifle is trained upon you; his dogs snarl.

"It was clever of you to go over the rocks," the captain says. "Perhaps it didn't occur to you that we would have dogs."

"Dogs," you repeat numbly. You are utterly dejected as the soldiers lead you and Simone down the mountain and place you in captivity with Jean-Paul and Marie.

The End

You take off across the mountain, your skis whisking through the snow. Raoul and Simone are close behind. You cross over the top of one ridge, but as you head down the slope, a huge crevasse suddenly looms before you. You stop just before you fall into its icy depths.

"We'll have to do a Tyrolean traverse," Simone calls, getting out her ropes.

"A Tyrolean traverse?" Raoul says.

"We rig a rope across the crevasse, then swing over to the other side," she explains quickly.

"We haven't got time," Raoul cries. "I know a way around it. Follow me!"

The white hoods of the Alpencorps are getting closer. You have to decide.

If you follow Raoul, turn to page 26.

If you decide to do the Tyrolean traverse, turn to page 28.

18

You decide it's better to avoid a confrontation before the mission even starts. Suddenly you dart into a doorway on your left.

You find yourself in the middle of a Moroccan kitchen. The family at the table breaks into an uproar. The children scatter, a man yells at you, and a dog growls menacingly.

"I'm very sorry," you say, holding up your hands to show you mean no harm. "Just passing through." You move quickly through the apartment and out the front door.

You have escaped this time, but now you have fair warning: Someone is on to you already. This will be your most difficult and dangerous mission yet.

Turn to page 8.

Dressed in your German uniforms, you and Simone cross the border with the aid of your false papers. By afternoon you're riding the tram that connects the town of Kliespitzen with Baderhoff Castle high in the valley. You leave the tram and descend a flight of stairs to the palatial central hallway of the castle. While you and Simone warm yourselves in front of a glowing fire, you try to get your bearings. Even with Raoul's map, it's not easy.

Then you remember the secret orders. De Grelle said to open them in the castle. While Simone studies the map, you take out the envelope and begin to read the note: "Believe Raoul—"

Suddenly a German officer walks up to the fire. "Cold outside, isn't it?" he says to you and Simone.

If you turn away and continue to read the note,
turn to page 74.

If you slip the note into your pocket,
turn to page 116.

The farmer seems innocent enough, and a warm meal and a bed for the night are too good to refuse. The three of you follow him home.

After a delicious country dinner, you settle into a feather bed for a good night's sleep. You are a little worried about how to get to Germany, but that problem can wait until morning.

In the middle of the night you are rudely shaken awake. Bleary-eyed, you are stunned to see Herr Kruptsch sitting next to your bed! His cold, small eyes bore into you. He draws his thin lips back in a smile.

"We meet again, my friend," he says, leaning toward you with a pistol. "You should know better than to trust old cars and new friends."

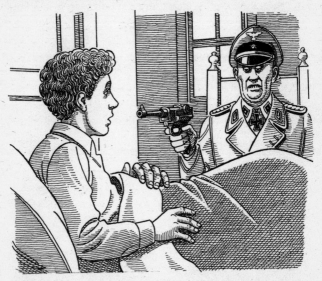

Turn to page 39.

"We'll give the German patrol boat all we've got before they even know what hit them," you tell the crew. "I'll give the command."

The crewmen ready their hidden weapons, and Simone hands you a few sticks of dynamite. You try to act nonchalant as the boat pulls up alongside the *Mermaid,* but every muscle in your body is tensed to attack. An ominous silence hangs over the boat.

The German captain regards you stonily. Suddenly he barks a command to his men. You will never know what gave you away—perhaps it was something in your eyes. But before you have a chance to lift a finger, their guns blow you out of the water.

The End

Marie swings the tank to the right. The road winds around and around the mountain on its way to the broad valley below. You're in luck. A whole division of tanks is rolling down the autobahn. It's the perfect cover.

Marie drives the tank up to the freeway and swings it neatly into last place in the line of tanks.

"We can go all the way to the front line in this convoy," you say happily. "From there we can split off from the rest and cross the border."

"If de Grelle could only see us now," says Simone. And all of you laugh.

The End

You follow the man through twisting, turning alleys you didn't know existed in Casablanca. Finally you arrive at a dark building with a low door.

"'My apartment," he says apologetically.

You look around apprehensively as he fumbles with the key. You do not know this part of the city. It is very quiet.

He opens the door and ushers you in. "I will turn on the light," he says.

Suddenly you sense the presence of others in the room. But before you can make a move, the door slams shut and your arms are pinned behind you. Someone chuckles in the dark, and you don't need a light to know who it is. It is Herr Kruptsch. How could you have fallen into such a trap? Your mission is over before it begins.

The End

You let the Kliespitzen train pass and wait for the express to Munich. An hour later you're racing through the Bavarian Alps. As you watch the snow-covered mountains go by, you try not to think about the risk you are taking by choosing Munich. So far Kruptsch has been one step ahead of you; this is your chance to outsmart him!

You and Simone step off the train in Munich. In the main lobby of the station you almost run smack into Marie and Jean-Paul! A Gestapo guard is on either side of them. You and your friends can barely hide your surprise, but luckily the Gestapo men don't notice.

You and Simone follow them at a short distance, conferring in a low whisper.

"Well, we made the right choice," Simone says. "The Gestapo must be pretty confident, putting only two men on them."

"I guess they figure they've fooled us, and they don't have to worry about anyone trying to rescue Jean-Paul and Marie in Munich," you reply. "Should we make a grab for them now?"

"It might be our only chance," says Simone. "But it also might be hard to escape in this crowd. Maybe we should follow them and hope we have a better opportunity later."

If you try to rescue your friends now, turn to page 14.

If you follow them and wait, turn to page 34.

Raoul breaks a trail uphill through the deep snow. It's hard work, and soon you're panting for breath as you wind between rock outcroppings and around snowbanks. A light snow begins to fall. The Alpencorps is no longer in sight, but you know the soldiers will be able to follow your tracks. You mention this to Raoul and Simone.

"What should we do?" Simone asks.

You survey the terrain. To your left is a rough rock rib of the mountain. Ahead is the top of a ridge.

"I think our best bet is to go to the top of this ridge," Raoul says. "We'll have fast skiing on the other side. It's downhill all the way to the castle."

You nod. "A downhill run would be a relief," you say. "On the other hand, the Alpencorps would still be able to follow our tracks. If we climb over the rocks, we may be able to lose them." But you cringe at the thought of dragging your exhausted body over the forbidding rocks.

In the quietly falling snow you hear the faint sound of German voices.

If you say, "I think we should climb over the rocks," turn to page 40.

If you say, "Let's take the downhill run," turn to page 66.

Marie maneuvers the tank onto the mountain road that climbs to Lieben. So far there is no pursuit; but if any comes, it will be no match for the tank.

You rumble up to the outskirts of Lieben and ditch the tank in the woods. "Switzerland is just over the mountain," you say.

"Since I speak German," Simone says, "I'll go into town and get us outfitted. Let's see—we'll need skis, packs, provisions, and extra clothing."

Marie goes along to help Simone carry everything back, and you and Jean-Paul wait anxiously in the woods. Finally they return, and you all gear up. Soon you are on your way through the forest and over the mountain to Switzerland.

The End

Attached to a rope, Simone rappels down into the crevasse. Then she uses her ice ax to climb up and out the other side. She anchors the rope on her side, and you anchor it on yours. With your skis stowed in your backpack, you grasp the rope firmly and swing across the great chasm, hand over hand. You feel your stomach drop as you dangle in midair. But you make it over safely, and Raoul follows.

Simone gathers up the rope and stows it in her pack. You thrust your boots into your ski bindings and make graceful telemark turns down the mountain. Looking back, you see the Alpencorps standing at the edge of the crevasse, dumbfounded.

You spend a freezing evening in a snow cave. The next day you ski over another ridge. Below you, nestled at the head of the Kliespitzen River Valley, is Baderhoff Castle. A tram and a tiny mountain road connect it to the town. But you have reached it by a more daring and unexpected route.

Dusk falls as the three of you arrive at the Nazi stronghold. You remove your skis and hide them in the nearby woods. You're chilled by the ice and wind, and the lights of the castle look inviting. But you have a strategic decision to make: Should you put on the German uniforms you have in your packs and use the forged transit papers to gain entrance? Or should you try to climb in through a window and rescue your friends by stealth? You also have the secret orders de Grelle gave you. Should you open them now?

If you want to go in disguised as a German officer, turn to page 37.

If you decide to enter through a window, turn to page 38.

If you think it's time to open the secret orders, turn to page 54.

30

"It's Kruptsch!" you say to Simone. "I'd recognize his voice anywhere."

"Kruptsch?" Michael echoes. "I know that name. We have carried out a few Resistance operations ourselves! Come, I will show you how to escape."

You and Simone dash out of the room behind Michael. "You can flee through the network of tunnels that runs underneath the monastery," he says. Then he has another thought. "Or you could disguise yourselves as monks and escape after Kruptsch leaves."

If you think the disguises will work, turn to page 120.

If you think the tunnels are your best bet, turn to page 130.

With one hand hanging on to your ice ax and the other desperately gripping Simone's wrist, you feel as if you'll be torn apart. Every muscle in your body strains to stay on the roof. Using reserves of strength you didn't think you had, you haul Simone up so that she can grab your ax with her free hand. Then you both lie there, clinging to the ax, gasping for breath.

Simone looks at you. "What now?"

Just then the window above you opens. You hope it is Jean-Paul or Marie.

"Who's there?" a man demands in German.

Whoever he is, he certainly isn't one of your friends!

If you remain motionless and hope you aren't seen, turn to page 62.

If you edge away from the window, turn to page 71.

The patrol boat pulls up alongside you. "Prepare to be boarded!" the German captain cries. He waves his submachine gun around as he steps onto the deck of the *Mermaid*. Raoul puffs on a pipe and Simone seems absorbed in mending a fishing net. The captain makes a quick search, kicking over buckets and upturning tarps, but he doesn't seem too interested in his task. For a tense moment he stops and glares at you; then he leaves abruptly without a word. Only when the patrol boat disappears into the distance do you breathe freely again.

You land on the French coast and bid farewell to the *Mermaid* and her crew. The leaky tub served you well after all.

One of Raoul's contacts in Marseilles has an old car waiting for you. The three of you begin the long trip through the French countryside. The road makes endless twists and turns through pastures and vineyards. It's a scenic route, but apparently the country roads are too much for the old car. As darkness falls it dies with a clunk.

Raoul gets out and looks at the mangled engine. "It will never start again," he announces.

You are stranded. Raoul hails a French farmer who happens to be passing by. When Raoul explains your car trouble, the farmer offers to help.

"Please accept my family's hospitality for the night," he says. "Our farm is just up the road."

It is getting dark and you are cold. But is it wise to accept his offer?

If you accept the farmer's offer, turn to page 20.

If you decide to keep going, turn to page 42.

You and Simone follow Jean-Paul, Marie, and the two Gestapo men out of the station. A black car is waiting for them at the curb. You hail a taxi.

"Follow that car," Simone tells the cabdriver. He looks at her as if she were crazy and says something about the Gestapo. The black car pulls away from the curb. There's no time to lose. Simone chops the cabbie on the neck and he goes limp. Then she jumps out, drags him onto the sidewalk, and takes the wheel.

Weaving in and out of traffic, she finally catches up with the Gestapo car at a light. When the signal changes, the black car accelerates quickly, but Simone stays right behind it. The driver pushes the Gestapo car faster, and still Simone stays with him. Suddenly the black car swerves wildly and smashes into a vegetable stand. You screech to a stop, jump out, and rush over to the car.

Turn to page 47.

You make camp on the side of the mountain and fall asleep quickly. The next morning you cross the gully safely, and Raoul leads you through the mountains. Finally you arrive on a ridge overlooking the Kliespitzen River valley.

Nestled at the head of the valley is Baderhoff Castle, where Marie and Jean-Paul are imprisoned. At the foot of the valley is the town of Kliespitzen, connected to the castle by a tramline and a narrow, twisting road.

Under cover of darkness you ski down to the castle. You stop in the woods nearby to consider your strategy.

"I have an idea," says Simone. "First, we sabotage the tram. That will create a diversion and disrupt traffic between the town and the castle. Then, in the confusion, we can rescue Jean-Paul and Marie."

You nod as you consider her plan. Silently you think about another option: You could take the time now to open the secret orders de Grelle gave you.

If you think you should open the secret orders, turn to page 54.

If you want to follow Simone's plan, turn to page 78.

Your German uniforms and false papers are accepted without question, and you walk through the doorway of the castle. Medieval tapestries, rare works of art, and gilded swords adorn the walls.

Simone leaves to scout out some escape routes while you and Raoul enter the palatial room where the German officers are gathering before dinner. You spot a table of appetizers and hungrily wolf down a handful. Raoul wanders off and strikes up a conversation with a handsome colonel. A few moments later he returns.

"That's Colonel Heinrich Richter," he says. "He has asked us to join him in his quarters for a private conversation."

You look over at the colonel and he smiles at you. There is something both appealing and frightening about his perfect good looks. Is he an ally or an enemy?

If you accept the invitation, turn to page 67.

If you refuse, turn to page 122.

"I can't say I like the idea of climbing through a window," says Raoul. "You know how I feel about heights. But I can show you where Jean-Paul and Marie are being held."

He leads you around to a remote wing of the castle and points to a window. It's perched at the top of a steeply pitched roof, at least sixty feet above the ground. A close look at the weathered stone wall shows that it has enough cracks and crevices to make a climb to the window possible. Simone gets out the gear.

"We'll climb up and lower Marie and Jean-Paul by rope," you tell Raoul. "You stay down here and catch them." He seems relieved that he doesn't have to make the climb.

With the aid of ropes and pitons, you and Simone scale the wall. The handholds are tiny and covered with ice. It is hard going. By the time you reach the roof you feel as if you can't climb another inch. But you can't go back now.

Turn to page 52.

So Kruptsch was behind the engine breakdown and the farmer's hospitality! He has been one step ahead of you all along. You have a sick feeling in the bottom of your stomach.

Kruptsch sits back in his chair. "Perhaps you would care to tell me what brings you to this part of France? You are not, after all, here on a ski vacation." His laugh is dry and forced.

You remain silent.

"Well," he says briskly, "we shall not waste time." A guard pushes Raoul and Simone into the room. "Either you begin to talk, or I will dispose of your friends—first one, then the other." He motions toward Simone, then Raoul.

If you refuse to talk, turn to page 48.

If you make up a story, turn to page 55.

If you think there is little to be lost by telling the truth, turn to page 59.

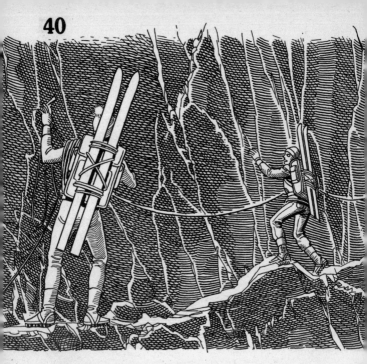

The three of you strap your skis to your packs, clamber onto the rocky rib, and begin the precarious traverse. The cold numbs your hands and feet. The snow, now falling heavily, cuts visibility to less than fifteen feet. The ice-covered rocks are slippery. But finally you make it to the end of the rib. A steep, snow-filled gully lies in front of you. You heave your packs off and sink into the snow, exhausted.

"I think we should make camp here," says Raoul. "It's getting dark and we need rest."

"I'm exhausted, too," says Simone. "But I'm also worried about the Alpencorps. If we push on across the gully, the snow will cover our tracks and we'll be doubly sure they won't find us."

Raoul eyes the gully. "I don't like the look of this snowfield. It could avalanche. It would be better to cross it in the morning, when we can see and the snow is more stable."

"True," says Simone, "but I think our first priority is to escape the Alpencorps."

Darkness is falling fast.

If you bivouac for the night, turn to pa

If you push on, turn to

There is something suspicious about the way the farmer showed up at just the right moment, so you say, "Thank you for your offer, but I think we'd better keep going." The farmer tips his hat and continues on his way.

You manage to hitch a ride on a truck going north. There is no room in the cab, so the three of you shiver in the back, trying to get some sleep as the truck drives through the night. At dawn you approach a town near the German border. You jump off the truck, and Raoul crumples to the ground in pain.

"My ankle!" he cries. "I think it's hurt pretty badly. What a stupid thing to do!"

You need to get help. Ahead of you is a town, where you could find a doctor for Raoul. To your right is a monastery, where you would not draw as much attention to yourselves.

If you take Raoul to the monastery, turn to page 49.

If you take him into town, turn to page 58.

The train to Kliespitzen pulls up. You and Simone board the coach and try to remain inconspicuous.

As the train chugs through the mountains, a thousand doubts run through your mind. The shock of Raoul's betrayal hasn't left you. Kruptsch seems to know everything about the mission, and what he doesn't know, Raoul will surely tell him.

The knots in your stomach tighten as the train pulls into the Kliespitzen station. You and Simone step out into the cold winter air. A man in a greatcoat sidles up to you and whispers in English, "You are here to rescue Marie and Jean-Paul?"

His question catches you off guard. You and Simone look at each other in bewilderment. But your hesitation has already given you away. The man shows you a Luger beneath his coat and smiles. "Kruptsch's description of you was perfect," he says. "Now you will come with me and join your friends for a little question-and-answer session."

The End

Raoul is still your best hope for completing the mission. Only he is familiar with the layout of the castle. But you vow to keep a close eye on him.

You walk back to Simone and Raoul. "Our next problem," you say, "is how to find Jean-Paul and Marie. How well do you know the castle, Raoul?"

"Like the back of my hand," he replies.

And now I know why, you think to yourself. Aloud you say, "Then we'll use our officers' uniforms and forged papers to get inside, and you can lead us from there."

Your disguises work perfectly, and soon you are walking through the awesome halls of Baderhoff Castle. But now that you are inside this Nazi stronghold, you're even more nervous about Raoul. Should you risk letting him lead you to Jean-Paul and Marie? You may not have time to reach them before he turns on you. Or should you try to get him to disclose their whereabouts, even though this may arouse his suspicions?

If you decide to ask Raoul to lead you to your friends, turn to page 72.

If you try to wheedle the information out of him, turn to page 124.

The figures in the snow seem harmless enough. Slowly you approach them and pull back the hoods of their parkas.

"Jean-Paul! Marie!" you exclaim.

Marie has barely enough strength left to open her eyes. But when she does, they light up. "A miracle!" she gasps. "How did you find us?"

"How did *you* get here?" you ask.

"We heard they were about to transfer us to Munich. So we used a couple of old tricks on a new guard to escape," she explains. "They came after us, but we lost them in the snow. Then we got lost."

"We called out for help in German, hoping to pass ourselves off as townspeople," puts in Jean-Paul. "Thank heaven you found us. We were near the end."

You bundle them up in extra clothes and give them food. Once you have revived them, you will have to start moving toward Switzerland to escape the Alpencorps.

The End

Jean-Paul and Marie are half-conscious but alive. You pull them from the wreckage and help them into the backseat of the taxi.

"Hey, what are you doing?" a bystander asks.

"Taking them to the hospital, you idiot!" Simone cries.

"What about the others?" says the bystander.

Simone just slams the door and speeds away. You examine Jean-Paul and Marie and find that they are bruised but otherwise unhurt.

"I took a risk," Marie manages to say. "I grabbed the driver's arm and made him crash." Then her eyes close.

"Shh," you say. "You need a rest. Don't worry, we'll get you out of here. We'll ditch the taxi somewhere, then head for the border. With our forged transit papers, we're practically home free."

The End

You look blankly at Kruptsch and keep your mouth shut. He waits impatiently, his frustration building.

Finally he bursts out, "Very well! Have it your way. Your silence will not last long. In the end you will wish you had talked to me rather than face my Gestapo friends in Baderhoff Castle."

The thought of Gestapo interrogation chills you. But at least you will be imprisoned in the same place as Jean-Paul and Marie. And who knows, perhaps there is still a chance. . . .

Your hands are bound, and two guards put you and Simone into the back seat of a black Mercedes. Kruptsch gets into the front seat. As the driver pulls away from the farmhouse, you demand, "What about Raoul? What are you doing with him?"

Kruptsch smiles mysteriously. "I wouldn't worry about Raoul."

You drive late into the night. At 2 A.M. you wake from a fitful sleep. The car is climbing the mountain road out of the town of Kliespitzen toward Baderhoff Castle. Simone and Kruptsch have dozed off.

You notice that the driver must slow down on the mountain curves. You might be able to open the door and leap from the car on one of these curves. But maybe you should wait until you reach the castle and make a break for it then.

If you try to escape now, turn to page 88.

If you decide to wait, turn to page 101.

You and Simone help Raoul hobble up the road to the monastery. You knock on the heavy wooden door. It opens with a creak to reveal a man in brown robes.

"Come in, come in," he says with a friendly smile. "I can see you are in need of help."

He introduces himself as Brother Michael. You explain you are farm workers heading south and that Raoul has hurt his ankle. Michael motions to some of the other monks, and they take Raoul upstairs.

"One of the brothers is skilled in medicine," Michael says. "Your friend will be in good hands. In the meantime, please join us for breakfast."

You settle down to a simple but hearty meal with the brothers. Suddenly there's a loud pounding at the door. "Open up!" a voice demands in German.

Turn to page 30.

Simone mixes with the officers in the dining room to try to find out where Jean-Paul and Marie are being held. You melt into the background.

Half an hour later she returns. "We just missed them," she says sadly. "Only a few moments ago they were taken from the castle to be transferred to Munich for further investigation."

Your spirits fall. If you can get out of the castle undetected, it's possible you can rescue Marie and Jean-Paul in Munich. But that is another mission.

The End

As you cling to the roof, waiting for the guards to pass, it occurs to you that you have not yet opened the secret orders. With your free hand you take out the envelope de Grelle gave you. You tear it open with your teeth and read the message inside:

> Believe Raoul is a double agent intending to betray you in the castle. Use your best judgment. Further instructions: sabotage castle if possible.
>
> *de Grelle*

You are still trying to absorb this revelation when the window above you opens. The cold voice of Herr Kruptsch chills you more than the ice on the roof ever could. "You can come in now, my friend. The games are over."

Turn to page 69.

On the roof you unrope, then use your ice axes to inch up the treacherous surface toward the window. Suddenly Simone slips and starts to slide down the roof! You thrust out your hand and grab her wrist. You stop her fall, but your arm feels as if it's about to be pulled off. You know you can only hold on a few more seconds.

"Let me go!" she gasps. "I'll try to catch the ledge of the roof. No point in both of us falling! You have to rescue Marie and Jean-Paul."

If you hold on and risk falling yourself, turn to page 31.

If you let her go and hope she can catch the roof ledge, turn to page 84.

You move away from Raoul and Simone, open the envelope de Grelle gave you, and read the message inside:

> Believe Raoul is a double agent intending to betray you in the castle. Use your best judgment. Further instructions: sabotage castle if possible.
> *de Grelle*

De Grelle must be right about Raoul—how else to explain the appearance of the Alpencorps the moment you landed behind German lines? You try not to show the shock you feel. The question is, How long should you trust him? Sooner or later he will betray you. But in the meantime, he may lead you to Jean-Paul and Marie.

If you decide you need Raoul a little longer, turn to page 45.

If you try to get rid of him right away, turn to page 106.

"There is no need to be unfriendly," you say to Kruptsch. "I'll tell you what I can, since you seem to know so much already." You tell him you're headed for southern Germany on a mission so secret you have not yet been told its ultimate purpose. "We are meeting an agent in Zurich who will give us further instructions."

Kruptsch sighs. "You are right about one thing: I already know the purpose of your mission. You intend to rescue your French Resistance friends from the Baderhoff Castle in the Bavarian Alps. As for the rest of your story—well, I have no time for lies." He levels his pistol at you.

The End

56

The farmer saddles the horses. You and Simone mount up, thank him, and ride into the fields. "Good luck," he calls after you.

The sun is rising over the horizon and the air feels fresh. You put the mission out of your mind for a few hours and enjoy the ride. But when you stop to let the horses graze, Simone points to a black Mercedes moving along the road.

"Kruptsch's car! He must have discovered our escape," she says. "I hope the farmer didn't suffer for it."

The car is coming your way. "He hasn't spotted us yet," you say, "but he will soon. We'd better move on."

You survey the terrain. Straight ahead is a fence with open fields beyond it and no road in sight. Kruptsch would have a hard time catching you there, but you'd have to jump the fence. To your right the land slopes down into a wooded glen. You can't see what is beyond the trees, but there are no fences to cross.

If you head for the fields, turn to page 95.

If you ride into the glen, turn to page 107.

You help Raoul hobble into town and find a doctor's office. The doctor is an old man with friendly wrinkles around his eyes. After he looks at Raoul's ankle, he says, "It's not serious, but it is broken. He'll have to stay off his feet for a couple of months."

When he leaves to attend another patient, the three of you confer.

"You *must* complete the mission," says Raoul. "I will draw you a map of the castle so you can find your way around without me."

Reluctantly you agree. The mission must come first. After Raoul has drawn you the map, you clap him on the shoulder. "Good luck," you say. "We'll meet back in Casablanca—with Jean-Paul and Marie." He smiles and waves goodbye.

Turn to page 19.

Perhaps there is some precious time to be gained by telling the truth. Kruptsch has been one step ahead of you from the beginning, so he probably knows it anyway.

Kruptsch smiles after you tell him your mission. "It is good that you are honest with me, my friend. It has spared your life for a little while." He tosses the pistol to Raoul. "Lock them in the barn. They must not escape."

You and Simone look at each other in shock. Raoul a traitor! Now you know how Kruptsch trapped you. But you have little time to ponder this because Raoul is pushing you out the door past an evil-looking black Mercedes that could only belong to Kruptsch.

"How could you, Raoul?" Simone cries. Raoul just sneers. He takes you to the barn and locks you inside. You can see no way out. The barn is cold and wet, and the straw pricks your skin. But at least you're alive.

Turn to page 63.

Somehow you find the strength to put on your skis and lift your pack back onto your aching shoulders. The gully and its dangerous snowfield loom before you.

"We'll cross one at a time," you say. "I'll go first."

You edge out into the gully. Gingerly you ski across, your eyes glued to the snow, your ears cocked for the telltale sounds of an avalanche. It seems to take ages to reach the other side. When you finally make it, you motion for Simone to follow. Once she's across, Raoul starts over.

Suddenly you hear a deep, ominous BOOM! Without warning, the ground gives way! Tons of moving snow pick you up and fling you head over heels down the mountain.

Turn to page 9.

You stay perfectly still and hold your breath. For a tense two minutes the man scans the night, but he doesn't see you. Finally he moves away from the window.

"Take the prisoners to the commandant," you hear him order someone inside. "If they still won't talk, we'll turn them over to Kruptsch." Then you hear a voice that makes your heart leap.

"Take your hands off me. I'm perfectly capable of walking by myself." It is Jean-Paul! You hear a shuffling of feet, followed by the slamming of a door.

Simone looks at you. "Should we wait for them to come back?"

"We can't stay out here all night," you answer. "If we could get to that chimney above the window, we could have a look around."

Turn to page 99.

Just before dawn the barn door opens. Is this the end? you wonder. But it is the farmer. "Quick!" he whispers. "You must escape. They forced me to do their will, and I may suffer for helping you. But you must complete your mission."

Surprised and grateful for this turn of events, you waste no time preparing to leave.

"Here is your equipment," the farmer says. "I can offer you either bicycles or horses to speed your escape. Unfortunately, I have no automobile."

If you take the horses, turn to page 56.

If you take the bicycles, turn to page 77.

You clamber through the window. Then, with all the speed your numb fingers can muster, you tie your rope to a bedstead in the room.

"You two rappel down first; I'll follow," you say. You let out the rope for Jean-Paul, then Marie. When she reaches the ground, Marie tugs on the rope to give you the go-ahead. You ease out the window. With the rope around your waist, you press your feet against the wall, lean out, and start down. Near the bottom, you feel a pull on the rope.

"Look out!" Jean-Paul calls.

You look up to see a guard cutting the rope. But he is too late. You are close enough to the ground to jump. Jean-Paul and Marie help you to your feet, and you escape into the woods. There you run into Simone. She is bruised and has one arm in a makeshift sling, but she's alive!

"Raoul broke my fall," she explains. "I got away with a broken arm. But he didn't survive." She looks away sadly.

"We'd better get going," you say. "They'll be after us any minute." You retrieve your gear from the woods, and the four of you head back into the mountains.

The End

While you rest over the next few days, you and Simone decide not to go on with the mission. Raoul is dead. You've lost your climbing equipment, German uniforms, and false papers. Reluctantly you set off for Switzerland.

You've only gone a few miles when you hear faint voices calling in German. You creep closer to the sounds and see two people floundering in the snow. Is it a trap, or are they really in need of help?

If you investigate the situation, turn to page 46.

If you decide you can't risk it, turn to page 70.

Raoul quickly skis up and over the ridge. When you and Simone reach the top, he is waiting twenty yards below. The snow, now falling heavily, makes it hard to see anything beyond him. He yells for you to come on down.

"Are you sure it's safe?" you call.

"Of course!" he answers. "I know this area perfectly."

"I don't like to ski places I can't see," Simone mutters.

But there is little time for debate. You turn your skis downhill and take off, with Simone right behind you. Raoul indicates where you should go. You zip past him . . . and there is nothing below you! You have skied over the edge of a thousand-foot cliff. As you fall through the air you wonder why Raoul had that strange smile on his face.

The End

Raoul must know what he's doing, you think as the two of you follow Richter to his room. You seat yourself in a plush baroque chair, noticing its eagle-claw feet.

"Something to drink?" Richter asks.

"No thanks," you say with a dry mouth. You hope the conversation doesn't get much more complex, or you'll soon be out of your league.

Raoul accepts a glass and lounges on the sofa. He seems completely at ease. Richter sits at his desk. "And how do you like our Baderhoff Castle?" he asks.

"Very much," you say.

"I'm so glad," he says in a voice that makes your blood run cold. "Because you and your French friends are going to be here for a long, long time—perhaps forever. Guards!"

The End

You'll have to rely on instinct and luck as you search Baderhoff Castle for Jean-Paul and Marie. "We've got two missions now," you say. "Rescue our friends and sabotage the castle. We'll have to work fast. Do you have the dynamite?"

Simone sets the time-delay fuses, and you hide bundles of explosives under couches and behind tapestries on your way to the wing where you think the prisoners are being held. The corridors are quiet, but you fear that at any moment Raoul will come around the corner.

Turn to page 82.

You have little choice but to do as he says. Once you're inside, Kruptsch eyes you with distaste. "It was lucky the guards overheard you talking with your friends," he says. "But your mission was doomed from the beginning." With de Grelle's message burning in your mind, you understand only too well what he means. He motions to two guards. "Take these three to my car."

The guards take you down to Kruptsch's black Mercedes. "Obviously your side knows where we've been keeping your friends," Kruptsch says, opening the car door. "So I think it is time we took a little trip."

"We *are* going on a trip, Herr Kruptsch. But we're going without you!" says a voice behind you. "Drop your weapons. I've got you covered." Everyone whirls around. It's Simone! You can't believe it.

After you tie up Kruptsch and his men, you notice her arm is in a makeshift sling. "How—?" you begin.

"I don't know. I guess Raoul broke my fall. A broken arm is all I got. He wasn't so lucky," she says sadly.

"It's the best thing that could have happened," you reply. Simone looks puzzled. "I'll explain on the way to the border," you say, stepping into the car.

The End

The figures in the snow may be decoys. You can't risk falling into a Nazi trap, so you pass them by.

This mission has been jinxed from the beginning, you think bitterly. The long trek through the mountains is ahead of you, and you can only hope the Alpencorps isn't lying in wait.

The End

Slowly, carefully, you move away from the window. You try not to make a sound. But you must use your ice ax to keep your hold on the slippery shingles.

The ax makes only the tiniest scraping noise. But that is enough. The man in the window fixes his gaze on you.

"There they are!" he cries.

Moments later a chorus of machine gun fire removes you and Simone from the roof in a very efficient manner.

The End

"Can you lead us to Jean-Paul and Marie right away, Raoul?" You hope the directness of your request will take him by surprise.

He's a little taken aback. "Sure, if that's what you think—"

"I think we shouldn't waste any time," you cut in.

Raoul takes you through the mazelike corridors of the castle to a quiet, remote wing. There you find a guard sitting at a table in front of a hallway. "They are down that corridor," he whispers to you. "Wait here."

He says something to the guard that you can't hear, then motions you to follow. That was too easy, you think. You'll have to put your cards on the table soon.

Raoul leads you to a room, turns the key, and pushes open the door. Jean-Paul and Marie are sleeping inside—but they can wait. Raoul's time has come. In one swift motion you grab his arm, twist it behind his back, and push him face first against a wall.

"Hey!" Raoul cries, struggling to get free.

Marie and Jean-Paul wake up, but their happy greetings are cut short by the strange scene in front of them. Simone looks puzzled too. You hand her de Grelle's note, and she reads it out loud.

"Now we know how the Alpencorps found us so fast," you say.

Raoul breaks down. "It's true—I've been working for the Gestapo. But I wasn't going to betray you. I was going to make sure you were safely away before I went to them. I want to defect," he pleads. "Let me join you. I will help you escape."

If you believe Raoul's story, turn to page 83.

If you do not believe him, turn to page 86.

You turn your back to continue reading, but someone grabs the note from behind. Before you can react, the officer has read de Grelle's secret instructions.

"Guards!" he calls. "Take away these spies!" You and Simone are immediately surrounded. It all happens so quickly that you are left stunned.

The officer hands the note back to you. "You won't be doing any sabotage around here," he declares.

You read the message:

> Believe Raoul is a double agent intending to betray you in the castle. Use your best judgment. Further instructions: sabotage castle if possible.
>
> *de Grelle*

Unfortunately, the information won't do you much good now that you're a prisoner.

The End

You find an open boxcar, and the four of you swing down into it, pulling the door closed behind you. It's a relief to be able to rest after the events of the past forty-eight hours. Soon everyone is asleep.

When you finally wake up, the train has stopped in the darkened railyard of a large city. "Where are we?" you wonder sleepily.

Cautiously, Simone gets out to take a look around. She returns a few minutes later and hops back into the boxcar. "According to the brakeman, we're in Hamburg," she says. "When he saw my uniform, he assumed I was a train guard."

"At least we're going in the right direction," you say. "I think we should stay put."

In a while the train chugs out of Hamburg. You put your eye to a crack in the door and watch the German villages pass in the night. Finally the train pulls into the port town of Rostock, on the Baltic Sea. There your false papers secure your passage on a boat to Sweden—and freedom, at last.

The End

You and the farmer wish each other luck. Then you and Simone speed away on the bicycles. The morning light begins to spread over the hills, the wind whips through your hair, and you feel lucky to be alive.

As the sun climbs into the sky, you look back. In the distance you see a black Mercedes with a swastika on its side. Kruptsch is on your trail! You zigzag through the hilly country, but Kruptsch is able to follow you—and he's getting closer. You pedal harder.

You're about to cross a one-lane bridge over a deep ravine when Simone suddenly stops. "Let's blow up the bridge," she says. "That will stop Kruptsch!"

You figure the Mercedes will catch up with you in less than two minutes. Is there time to plant the charges?

*If you decide to dynamite the bridge,
turn to page 90.*

*If you think you don't have time,
turn to page 97.*

"Let's sabotage the tram," you say.

Taking care to stay hidden in the trees, you go around to the front of the castle. About two hundred meters below you, perched on a rocky hillside, is one of the tram towers.

"Can you bring down that tower?" you ask Simone.

"No problem," she says.

"Good. Then let's go do it. Raoul, you stay here. We'll return as soon as we set the charges. Then you can take us into the castle."

Raoul nods his assent, and you and Simone move stealthily down to the tower. Simone implants the fuses in the dynamite, and you help her rig it to the crucial stress points of the tower. When everything is in place, you run back to your meeting point. But Raoul is not there. He has disappeared!

Turn to page 126.

"Quick! Onto the roof!" you cry. You leap onto the roof of the tram car, and it moves out into the icy night. Your fingers turn numb as you cling desperately to the cable. You just hope the tram will make it to the bottom of the mountain before Raoul breaks through the steel doors of the control room and stops the car.

Just as the car is nearing the bottom of the mountain, it stops. Raoul *has* broken through the doors. But luck is with you. You are close enough to the ground to jump to safety.

You wade through the snow into the town of Kliespitzen, where you and Simone—still in your officers' uniforms—commandeer an army truck. You pick up Jean-Paul and Marie, and head for Switzerland and freedom. As you drive out of town, several flashes light up the sky. Simone's explosives have done their job.

The End

"If you can't give me the information here and now, I don't want it," you say to the man.

He looks down.

"If you want to meet me at the Café Paris tomorrow, I'll be glad to talk there," you offer.

"I c-can't do that," he says.

"Then we're just wasting time," you say firmly. You turn abruptly and walk away. But once you get back to your room, you don't feel so confident. What if the man *did* have vital information? If nothing else, you have learned that you and your friends are not the only ones who know about this mission. You spend a restless night turning this over in your mind.

Turn to page 8.

You search the wing farthest from the one Raoul said housed the prisoners. On a hunch you go down a narrow corridor until you see a guard at a table in front of a hallway. "I'll bet this is it!" you whisper to Simone.

You knock out the guard, take his keys, and enter the hallway. Then you unlock the first door—and there are Jean-Paul and Marie. They are overjoyed to see you.

"We have to get out of here fast," you say. "It won't be long before they come after us."

You race up to the tram room and take the first car down the mountain. As you come out of the tram station in town, someone cries, "There they are!"

A platoon of soldiers races toward you. The four of you flee down the street to a bridge over railroad tracks. Frantically you look for a means of escape.

Simone spots a motorcycle with a sidecar parked next to the bridge. "The keys are still in it!" she cries.

You start toward the motorcycle; then you catch sight of a freight train coming down the tracks. It is moving slowly, so you could jump onto its roof from the bridge.

If you decide to jump onto the train, turn to page 102.

If you'd rather take the motorcycle, turn to page 108.

82

In a remote part of the castle you find a guard seated at a table in front of a hallway. This could be the place. You and Simone take a calculated risk. Simone produces a bottle of schnapps—a peppermint-flavored liqueur—and motions that she is going to take it to the guard. You wait behind a corner.

Simone starts up a lively conversation with the guard. She gets him to drink the schnapps, and you slip down the hallway when he's not looking. Jean-Paul and Marie greet you eagerly through the grate in their door. Your instincts were right!

Simone comes down the hall with the key. "The guard went out like a light." She laughs. "After he had a few drinks, it wasn't hard to knock him over the head."

You release your friends and, after a brief but joyous reunion, retrace your steps through the castle. You are just beginning to think you eluded Raoul when you hear footsteps behind you.

Turn to page 91.

"Okay," you say, releasing Raoul. "I'll give you another chance. Lead us out of here. But don't forget, I'll be watching every move you make."

"You won't be sorry," he says, rubbing his arm. "There's an elevator in the back of the castle that's hardly ever used. We can take it down to the loading dock, and from there I can get us a truck to escape in."

The four of you follow Raoul to the elevator. He loads you in quickly, and the car drops. When the doors open at the bottom, eight Gestapo men are waiting with machine guns.

"I seem to have changed my mind," Raoul says with a grin.

The End

84

Reluctantly you release Simone's hand. She slides down the roof and catches the ledge. But she's unable to get a solid grip on the ice. You must watch in silent horror as she falls off the roof—and lands right on top of Raoul!

You stare at your two friends on the ground. Neither moves. You want to give up, but now more than ever you feel you must complete the mission.

You move up the roof carefully, your hands numb from the cold. At last you reach the window and slowly raise your head above the ledge. Your heart leaps. Jean-Paul and Marie are inside! You tap on the pane. Marie's baffled look turns to amazed delight when she opens the window. But she quickly puts her finger to her lips.

"Shh," she whispers. "We heard the guards talking. I think they are about to check on us."

If you say, "I'll hold on till the guards pass,"
turn to page 51.

If you say, "I can't stay out here any longer,"
turn to page 64.

"Thanks, but no thanks," you say to Raoul. "Whether you like it or not, we're going to follow your first plan. You let us get away, then you can do whatever you want. And just to make sure you don't betray us—" You tie him up tight and gag him.

You turn to the others. "Let's go. The Gestapo will be here any minute." The four of you rappel out the window and retrieve your gear from the woods. You have a comfortable jump on the Alpencorps as you head for Switzerland.

The End

You and Simone dash up the stairs two steps at a time, fighting a steady stream of people pouring out of the burning castle. You search the second floor in vain.

"Let's try the third floor!" you yell to Simone.

You run up another flight. Your lungs are on fire from the smoke. Frantically you check every room. Suddenly you hear a shout from a room down the hall. "Help! We're locked in!"

"It's Marie!" Simone cries.

You rush to the door and kick it with all your might. Finally you break through, and Jean-Paul and Marie fall into your arms, nearly overcome by smoke. Simone starts to lead them down the hallway.

"Wait!" you cry. "If you've still got your ropes, Simone, our best bet is to escape out the window."

"What about Raoul?" Simone asks, quickly rigging up the rope.

You can feel the heat of the fire getting closer. "We haven't got time to find him. We'll just have to hope he can take care of himself."

The four of you rappel out of the castle. In the confusion on the ground you manage to steal a German staff car. You get stuck in the traffic jam leaving the castle, but you know that with a little patience it won't be long before you reach the border.

The End

Using your teeth, you pull up the door lock. Then you turn so that your bound hands are on the handle, nudge Simone awake with your knee, and whisper, "Get ready to jump!" As the driver brakes for a curve, you jerk open the door and tumble out of the car. Simone is right behind you.

Luckily the snow at the edge of the road cushions your fall. You get up and dash into the forest. Although Kruptsch was fast asleep when you made your leap, you're sure it won't be long before he's after you.

A few minutes later, out of breath from stumbling through the snow, you stop.

"I don't hear anything," Simone says. "They're not chasing us."

"Of course," you say thoughtfully. "They don't need to come after us now. Here we are in the

snow and cold with no provisions. They'll figure we can't get far. At dawn they'll simply send out a very methodical search party."

"Which means," Simone says, "we'd better cover a lot of ground before dawn—and before we freeze to death."

You and Simone use sharp rocks to cut the ropes binding your hands. Then you consider your options. If you go into town, you can get food and warm clothing. But Jean-Paul and Marie are in the castle, and it's the last place Kruptsch would look for you.

If you set off for Baderhoff Castle, turn to page 111.

If you head toward Kliespitzen, turn to page 121.

90

Simone's skilled fingers rig the explosive on the crucial stress points of the bridge. She sets a short fuse. "Let's get out of here!" she cries.

As you jump on your bikes and start across the bridge, Kruptsch's car screeches around the corner—and stops short. He must have guessed what you are up to.

You tear across the bridge, racing the fuse. But your tire hits a rock and you skid to the ground. Simone doesn't see you and continues across. You pick yourself up and jump back on the bike, but you fear it may be too late.

You are right. The dynamite blows while you are still on the bridge. The pavement crumbles beneath you. You can only hope Simone will finish the mission by herself.

The End

"Halt!" a voice yells. It is Raoul with several guards. You dash down the hallway and up countless flights of stairs, two steps at a time. You are headed for the tram room at the top of the castle. It is your best hope of escape. Raoul and the guards are close behind.

You burst into the tram room, panting for breath. Marie and Jean-Paul bar the steel door behind them. Simone goes to the control box and starts the motor. The empty tram car begins to move out of the room without you and your friends!

If you risk jumping onto the roof of the tram car, turn to page 79.

If you try to stop the car and bring it back into the room, turn to page 96.

"Marie has a good point," you say. "Let's hijack the train."

You leap from boxcar to boxcar, leading your companions to the roof of the engine. "We'll take the engineer by surprise," you say. "I'll swing down to the cab on this side. Simone, you swing down on the other side. If we need help, we'll call for you, Jean-Paul and Marie." You position yourselves at the edge of the roof. "Now!" you cry.

You and Simone swing over and burst into the cab. The engineer is completely taken by surprise. You pin him to the wall while Simone takes care of his assistant.

"All clear," you call to your friends.

They swing down and join you. "What do we do now that we have ourselves a train?" Jean-Paul asks.

You consult the engineer's map. "I see a route for us. We can follow the Rhine for a while, then cut west to the border, where we can abandon the train. From there we'll travel cross-country to the Dutch coast and get help from one of our contacts in Rotterdam."

You push the train up to top speed and barrel down the tracks.

The End

You run down the hallway to your left. The castle is a mass of confusion. You push desperately through the crowd, with Simone right behind you.

You search every corridor and every room, but there is no sign of your friends in that wing of the castle. The smoke thickens, and you start to cough uncontrollably.

"If they haven't escaped by now, there's no hope for them," Simone manages to choke out.

The same goes for you. You turn back toward the front door. But you can make little headway in the mayhem. Suddenly the hallway is engulfed by flames. You and Simone succumb with the rest of the trapped inhabitants of Baderhoff Castle.

The End

"We'll have to get a good run to clear that fence," you say. You dig your heels into the horse's sides and shout, "Giddyup!"

The horse gallops toward the fence, and you brace yourself for the jump. But suddenly he stops short! You are pitched forward over his head and into the railing. You hear a crack, and a sharp pain shoots up your leg.

Simone rides over to help you. She takes one look at your leg and says, "We'll have to get a doctor, quick!"

It looks as if you'll be spending the next few months in the French countryside, recuperating from a broken leg.

The End

"Stop the tram!" you cry.

Simone pulls the lever to STOP, then RE-VERSE, and the car slides back into the room. You and your friends pile inside, and she pushes the lever forward to full throttle. Then she races over to the door, and you pull her in.

Breathing hard, she says, "I just hope we make it to the bottom before Raoul and the guards break into the control room."

You have just passed the tower halfway down the mountain when the tram jerks to a halt. You look out the window. There are 200 feet between you and the ground. "One thing's for sure," you say. "We can't jump from here."

"What will happen to us now?" asks Jean-Paul.

His question is soon answered. The tram starts moving again—only now it's going back up the mountain toward Raoul and his men. And you are powerless to stop it.

Turn to page 114.

"We don't have time to mine the bridge," you say. You spot some old wine bottles by the side of the road. "But maybe these will stop Kruptsch."

You break the bottles and spread the jagged pieces across the front edge of the bridge. Then you jump on your bikes and pedal hard.

Kruptsch comes speeding around the corner and hits the bridge at full tilt. You hear a loud BANG as his tires hit the broken glass, then a CRUNCH as the car hits the side of the bridge. Kruptsch jumps out and fires his gun at you. But you are out of range.

You stick to the back roads for the rest of the trip to Germany. When you reach the border two days later, you leave the bikes in the woods, put on your German uniforms, and walk up to the border guard.

Turn to page 110.

With painstaking slowness you manage to reach the chimney. From there you scan the sea of gables and parapets around you. A light shines from a skylight a few meters away. Leaving the rope at the chimney, you straddle a pointed gable and make a precarious traverse over to the flat top of a parapet. Simone follows behind. Cautiously you peer inside.

You jerk back instantly. "It's Jean-Paul and Marie!" you whisper. "They're being interrogated!"

If you and Simone drop through the skylight, you'll certainly put an end to the questioning. But you'll have to take on the German guards. Would it be wiser to make a less dramatic entrance through an unguarded window?

If you jump through the skylight, turn to page 113.

If you look for another entrance to the castle, turn to page 128.

You rein your horses into the glen and hide behind some bushy fir trees. "Shh, shh," you whisper, patting your restless mount's neck.

The black car tears around the corner, and Kruptsch doesn't even glance in your direction as he goes speeding by.

"Whew!" Simone says. "That was close."

"It sure was," you say. "Let's stick to the woods and fields from now on."

You turn the horses back toward the open fields and set off for Germany. You avoid the roads and camp out at night. Two days later you reach the border. You leave the horses in a farmer's field, with a note tied to their saddles explaining to whom they belong. Then you don your German uniforms and walk up to the border crossing.

Turn to page 110.

When you arrive at the castle, a heavy guard is waiting to take you inside. It would be insane to try to break free now. You let the men take you to your cell, where you spend a miserable week not knowing your fate or that of your friends.

Finally Kruptsch visits your cell. "You have been very useful to us," he says. "We have negotiated a secret exchange of prisoners with your Colonel de Grelle. Originally we planned to exchange your two French Resistance friends for two of our agents. Unfortunately, they escaped about the time we captured you."

You and Simone can barely hide your glee. That was a week ago, and it's obvious that Jean-Paul and Marie have not been recaptured!

"However," Kruptsch continues, "you two will do just as well for the exchange. In fact, you'll do better. De Grelle is now willing to return *three* of my men."

You wish Kruptsch weren't getting his agents back because of you. But you're happy that your friends are free, and you and Simone vow to get Kruptsch next time.

The End

The four of you line up on the bridge. The train chugs underneath. "Now!" you yell. All of you leap.

The jump is perfectly timed, and everyone lands safely. You press yourselves flat against the roof of the boxcar just as the Germans reach the bridge and fire a rain of bullets on you. But soon you are out of their range.

"Where is this train taking us?" Jean-Paul wonders.

"It looks as if we're headed north," you reply.

"So are we just going to stow away until we find a good place to get off?" Simone asks.

"We don't have to do that," says Marie. "We could take over the train."

"That sounds risky," Jean-Paul objects.

"I don't think it's any more risky than stowing away," Marie says. "Who knows where the train might take us?"

If you think you should stow away, turn to page 75.

If you favor Marie's plan, turn to page 92.

Neither of you speaks as you take the left passage. Somehow you feel you can't make noise down here.

You walk on and on. In the darkness and silence you begin to feel as if you are suspended in space, almost as if you do not exist. The outside world ceases to matter. Your senses are numb.

Suddenly there is nothing under your feet. You and Simone drop through the air.

"Whoops," says Simone.

It's the last thing you hear.

The End

You push Raoul into a vacant bathroom and lock the door behind you both. You're on your guard, in case he decides to jump you. Instead it seems as if he's going to talk you to death. Over and over he protests that he's innocent and that he can be trusted.

Time drags on and eventually Raoul is reduced to sullen silence. Finally Simone returns. She looks discouraged.

"Sorry I was away so long," she says. "But I had to be very careful whom I talked to and what I said."

"What did you find out?" you ask.

"Jean-Paul and Marie *aren't* here," she says with a sigh.

"What did I tell you?" Raoul crows.

"But they *were*," Simone says with a glare. "Up until about fifteen minutes ago. It turns out that while I was being so discreet, Kruptsch was parading our friends right through the castle!" She sighs. "They've been transferred to Munich."

So things are no clearer than before. All you can do is take Raoul back to Casablanca. Maybe there you can sort out the mess and regroup for another rescue attempt.

The End

106

You must get rid of Raoul without making him suspicious. "Here's the plan," you say. "Simone and I will go around to the other side of the castle and try to climb in secretly. Raoul, I know you don't like heights. So you go into town and find us a getaway car. We'll meet back here in six hours."

He agrees and you watch him head toward town, making sure he doesn't double back. Then you show de Grelle's note to Simone.

"This is incredible!" she exclaims.

"I know it's hard to believe," you say. "But it means we must work fast. I'm sure Raoul will go straight to the Gestapo once he reaches town—which is why we're not going to follow the plan I just gave him. Instead, we'll use the German uniforms and forged papers to get into the castle. If we work fast enough, we can rescue Marie and Jean-Paul before Raoul catches up to us."

In your disguises, you have no problem gaining entrance to the castle. But once inside, you realize what a huge place it is. Your footsteps echo off the high ceilings. You feel very small.

You see a large room where German officers are milling about before dinner. Should you risk having Simone make discreet inquiries about Jean-Paul and Marie? Or should you trust your instincts to find the place where they're being held?

If you decide Simone should make inquiries,
turn to page 50.

If you go directly to look for Jean-Paul and Marie,
turn to page 68.

The glen is a tangle of trees, bushes, and brambles. Somewhere below, you hear a river flowing. You manage to struggle free of the brambles and ride down an embankment. You come out onto a road that curves along the river.

"This is a peaceful scene," Simone says. "But I'm afraid we may meet up with Herr Kruptsch if we stay here. It's hard to see what is around these curves."

At that moment you hear a screech of tires. It's Kruptsch, coming around the bend!

If you duck back into the trees to elude Kruptsch, turn to page 100.

If you try to escape by crossing the river, turn to page 125.

Simone hops on the motorcycle behind you, and your companions squeeze into the sidecar. You rev up the engine, kick it into gear, and take off. A host of vehicles pursues you through the streets of Kliespitzen and out onto the open highway.

The road twists wildly down the mountain. You wheel around the curves, pushing the motorcycle to its limits. But the cars behind you draw closer.

As you descend into rolling farmland, you realize your pursuers will catch up with you in a matter of seconds. In a desperate move, you veer off the road, burst through a wooden fence, and speed across the rolling pastures. The motorcycle bounces crazily on the rough ground. But you manage to keep your balance, and your passengers hold on for dear life. When you've put some distance between yourself and the road, you look back. The soldiers are standing at the edge of the pasture, totally confounded.

The End

Your false papers get you over the border. But you begin to have second thoughts about your plan of action. You voice them to Simone as you wait at the depot for a train to Kliespitzen. That is the town nearest Baderhoff Castle, where your friends are being held.

"We've shaken Kruptsch off our trail, but that doesn't mean we've heard the last of him," you say. "He knows about our mission. What if he calls the castle and has Jean-Paul and Marie transferred?"

Simone thinks for a moment. "Well," she says, "if they *are* transferred, they will almost certainly be taken to Gestapo headquarters in Munich."

"So if they're not at the castle, we go to Munich," you say.

"I don't think we have time for both before Kruptsch and Raoul catch up with us," Simone replies. "We have to choose one or the other and hope we choose right!"

If you go to Munich, turn to page 24.

If you go to the castle, turn to page 43.

The night is bitterly cold. As you slog through the snows, you sense that you are in a valley. You can only hope it leads to the castle. In any case, you have no choice but to push on as fast as your straining lungs will allow.

After a couple of hours you're ready to drop. Your feet are soaked, your hands are frozen, and there is no sign of the castle. But Simone reminds you that dawn is not far off, and that spurs you on.

As the first gray light of day touches the mountain, you look up from your steady slogging to see two figures coming toward you. Quickly you grab Simone's arm and hide behind a snowdrift.

"Who are they?" you whisper. "They don't seem to be armed, and they're not wearing uniforms. But who would be out here at a time like this?" You hold your breath and wait.

Go on to the next page.

The figures come closer, and you recognize them. "Jean-Paul! Marie!" you cry, rushing out to greet them. It seems impossible, but it's true.

After the happy reunion Jean-Paul explains, "We broke out of the castle, but we didn't know where to go. We've been wandering in the woods all night."

"One thing is for sure," you say. "We can't stay in this valley. It will be crawling with search parties soon. Simone and I escaped from Kruptsch only a few hours ago."

"I have an idea," Marie says. "Why don't we go up to the road? It's the last place they would expect us to be, and maybe we can ambush a car."

Jean-Paul looks skeptical, but the rest of you are already hiking up toward the road. You hide behind a snowbank just above the road, and soon you can hear the rumble of something big coming around the corner.

"Great," Jean-Paul mutters, "they're sending a whole battalion after us."

You peer over the snowbank and see a tank.

"Perfect!" says Marie. "What better way to escape than in a tank?" Jean-Paul and Simone look at her as if she were crazy, but you wonder if her idea might not work.

If you think you can take the tank, turn to page 118.

If you decide to wait for something smaller to come down the road, turn to page 132.

In a single, smooth motion, you open the sky-light, drop through it, and land on the commandant. The force of your jump knocks him out. As a captain moves to seize you, Simone jumps through and knocks him out. In the meantime, Jean-Paul and Marie turn on the surprised guards and disarm them.

"Are we glad to see you!" Marie says.

"Just thought we'd drop in," you say with a grin.

Someone leaps out of a corner and attacks you with a scream. Marie and Jean-Paul grab him and wrestle him to the ground.

"Raoul!" you cry in surprise.

"He's in with them," Jean-Paul says in disgust. "When he saw that you and Simone had reached the roof safely, he came to tell the commandant how to catch you."

Raoul glares at you, but you don't have time to waste on him. You tie him up and lock him in a closet while Simone retrieves the rope from the chimney. Then the four of you climb out the window, rappel down the wall of the castle, and make off into the alpine night.

The End

As your tram car approaches the halfway tower, Simone's explosives detonate in the castle in a series of thunderclaps. The electricity goes out. The tram stops.

You climb onto the roof of the car and gauge the distance between you and the tower. "Hand me a rope," you call to Simone. "I'm going to jump to the tower."

You clench one end of the rope in your teeth. Simone holds on to the other end. Then you take a deep breath—and leap.

The impact with the tower knocks the breath out of you. But you're able to cling to the metal structure. You find a place to anchor the rope securely, and one by one your friends swing over from the tram and climb down the tower.

In the confusion that follows the explosions, you have no trouble escaping to Kliespitzen, where you commandeer a car for your journey to the border.

The End

You smile politely at the officer, but you keep your mouth shut, trusting Simone to handle the situation.

"It certainly *is* cold out," Simone says to the officer. Casually she puts the map in her pocket.

"Did you just arrive?" he asks.

"Yes," she replies. Her voice sounds a little nervous.

"Why not join me for dinner, then? I'll show you around the place."

"Thank you," Simone says politely, "but we already have plans."

The officer tips his hat and moves away.

"Narrow escape," Simone murmurs to you.

You read the rest of de Grelle's note:

> Believe Raoul is a double agent in-
> tending to betray you in the castle. Use
> your best judgment. Further instruc-
> tions: sabotage castle if possible.
>
> *de Grelle*

"Raoul a double agent? Incredible!" Simone exclaims when you show her the message. "That means we can't trust his map."

"Exactly," you say. "And that's why we won't follow his instructions. In fact, we'll go to the opposite side of the castle."

Turn to page 81.

You can't imagine breaking the underground silence. Without a word you lead Simone to the right.

Carefully placing one foot in front of the other, you move forward. Soon you forget you are walking. In the darkness and silence you feel as if you are floating in outer space. Your head feels light.

After a while you begin to feel a strange joy. A few minutes later you come to the sudden realization that you can see the outline of Simone's head. Light! Slowly the light increases as you walk on. Finally you reach a ladder that leads up into the blinding daylight.

Strengthened by your ordeal, you and Simone head for Germany to complete your mission, while Kruptsch searches fruitlessly for you in the monastery.

The End

"Let's take the tank," you say to Jean-Paul and Simone. "Once we're inside, no one will be able to stop us."

As the tank passes by, the four of you jump over the snowbank and land on top. Simone knocks on the hatch. "Open up," she cries in German.

The hatch opens. No sooner does the commander's head poke out than three of you grab him by the shoulders and hurl him off the tank. You do the same to the next man who appears. Then you all pile into the tank and shut the hatch. Marie takes the controls.

"We're invincible in this thing!" you exclaim. You roll into town without any problem, but as you're leaving you run into a roadblock. An officer tries to flag you down.

"We're done for if we stop," Jean-Paul says.

"Keep going," you say, waving cheerfully at the officer through the tiny window.

Marie puts the tank into high gear and barrels straight into the roadblock. The Germans open fire, but their bullets bounce harmlessly off the steel tank. You push the roadblock aside as if it were cardboard and roll down the road at top speed.

In a few miles you come to a fork. A sign tells you that the left fork climbs to the mountain town of Lieben. From there you could cross into Switzerland. The road on the right descends to an autobahn, or freeway. The military traffic that travels on it would make a good cover for your escape.

If you go right, turn to page 22.

If you go left, turn to page 27.

You barely have time to put on the monks' habits and slip the cowls over your heads before Kruptsch bursts into the dining room. "Search this place from top to bottom," you hear him order his men.

You and Simone enter the dining room with Michael, your heads bowed.

"I really must protest—" Michael starts to say.

"Shut up!" Kruptsch commands. Soon his men return from their search, empty-handed.

"Who are they?" Kruptsch demands, pointing at you and Simone.

"Just two of the brothers," Michael says calmly. "They have taken vows of silence."

"I see," Kruptsch says. Abruptly he motions for his men to leave with him. You let out a sigh of relief.

Suddenly Kruptsch turns and barks out your name. Involuntarily your head jerks up. You recover quickly, but it's too late! Kruptsch was watching you closely. His men seize you and Simone.

The End

You make your way as fast as you can through the deep snow in the dark. Luckily, you're going downhill. When you reach town you take shelter in a woodshed. Cold and wet, you begin to wonder about your mission.

Simone echoes your thoughts when she says, "How are we going to finish the mission?"

"I don't know," you answer. "We've lost our equipment, our disguises, and our forged papers. We've lost Raoul. We're exhausted and on the verge of frostbite."

The more you think about it, the more you realize that it would be foolhardy to go on. You decide to try to make your way through France back to Casablanca. There you can consult de Grelle and try again.

The End

Raoul goes off to make your excuses to the colonel. Once again you remember the secret orders de Grelle gave you. They may contain vital information, you think as you tear open the envelope. But you never expected this!

Believe Raoul is a double agent intending to betray you in the castle. Use your best judgment. Further instructions: sabotage castle if possible.

de Grelle

BELIEVE RAOUL IS
A DOUBLE AGENT
INTENDING TO BETRAY
YOU IN THE CASTLE.
USE YOUR BEST
JUDGMENT.
FURTHER INSTRUCT-
IONS: SABOTAG
CASTLE IF
POSS

Go on to the next page.

Simone returns and you show her the note. She lets out a low whistle of amazement. "It's hard to believe," she says. "But it explains how the Alpen-corps found us so quickly in the mountains. Why didn't de Grelle tell us right away?"

"Because he didn't want us to let on that we were suspicious," you reason. "And we needed Raoul to guide us to the castle. But I'm not sure if we can trust him to lead us to Jean-Paul and Marie. He may turn on us at any moment."

"I could make some discreet inquiries among the officers and see if they know where the prisoners are kept," Simone suggests. "Or we could trust our instincts and just start looking."

If you want Simone to make inquiries, turn to page 50.

If you decide to start looking right away, turn to page 68.

If you are subtle enough, you may get Raoul to tell you where to find Jean-Paul and Marie. You pull him and Simone into a small room off the hall. "Let's plan our strategy," you say. "Where do you think our friends are being held, Raoul?"

"The prisoners are kept in a remote wing of the castle," he says, sketching a rough map on a piece of paper. He looks up at you. Suddenly there's suspicion in his eyes. "Why don't I just lead you there?" he demands.

"Because you are a traitor!" you reply. In a single quick motion you pin his arms behind his back before he has a chance to resist.

Simone looks shocked.

"Who told you that?" Raoul demands. "De Grelle?"

"What does it matter?" you ask.

"It matters because it's de Grelle who's the traitor. This mission is a fake! It's a setup to trick you into getting rid of me! I'll bet anything Jean-Paul and Marie aren't even here. They never were."

You begin to have doubts. *What if he's right?* Your head spins as you try to figure out who is double-crossing whom.

Turn to page 131.

You've got to get to the river! Like a bolt of lightning you take off down the road, with Simone right behind you. Kruptsch's car accelerates to catch you.

The road takes a sharp turn to the right. You rein your horses to the left, crash through the reeds, and splash into the river. Kruptsch's brakes screech as he loses control of the car on the turn. The car skids off the road, flips over once, and lands in the river.

You and Simone swim your horses across the river. You pull yourselves up on the far bank and stand dripping as Kruptsch's car disappears beneath the surface of the water. With him out of the way, you are confident you will complete your mission.

The End

The dynamite explodes in a series of bright flashes. The tram tower topples to the ground, bringing the cables with it. One of the tram cars plunges from the castle and lands directly on a gas-storage tank. The tank explodes in an enormous burst of flame. You are knocked to the ground. This is more than you bargained for!

When you pick yourself up, the castle is in flames. "We've got to find Raoul and save Jean-Paul and Marie!" you cry.

You rush into the castle with Simone. People are running in every direction. You try to see your way through the smoke. There's a staircase in front of you and a hallway to your left. You can only guess where your friends are.

If you run up the staircase, turn to page 87.

If you take the hallway, turn to page 94.

You and Simone search all over the rooftop, but you can't find anyplace to enter undetected. Frustrated, you use your ice axes and ropes to cross the sea of gables and parapets to the front part of the castle. There you rappel down a thirty-foot wall to a flat roof below. Suddenly a familiar voice drifts up from the darkness.

"That's Kruptsch!" you whisper.

Simone grabs your arm and points straight down. There you see your archenemy approaching his black Mercedes. Two guards are with him—and so are Marie and Jean-Paul!

"Let's rappel down and get them," you say excitedly.

"Wait," Simone says, pulling you back down. "I've got a better idea. We'll bean Kruptsch from up here. *Then* we'll go down and save them." She searches through her climbing supplies, pulls out a supply of carabiners, and hands a couple to you. You each take careful aim at Kruptsch and throw at the same time. The carabiners miss and clank harmlessly on the concrete below. Kruptsch and the guards look around in confusion. Again you and Simone take aim. This time you both hit your target. Kruptsch crumples to the ground—out cold.

"Now for the guards," Simone says. She lights two sticks of dynamite and flings one to the left and one to the right. The explosions confuse the guards even more, and they run off to investigate, forgetting about Jean-Paul and Marie.

Go on to the next page.

You and Simone seize your chance. You rappel down the wall and run to Kruptsch's car. Marie has already started the engine, and Jean-Paul holds the door open for you.

"Get in!" Marie says happily. "I thought you two might be behind this!" She takes off down the road for the border.

The End

130

Michael lifts up a rug, uncovering a trap door that leads into the tunnels. You and Simone climb down a long ladder into the inky darkness below. Before he closes the door, Michael tosses down a flashlight. "You'll need this," he says. "Good luck!"

"Thanks!" you call back.

You make your way through the passage. The flashlight barely penetrates the heavy darkness. The walls are dank and covered with something slippery. Occasionally you pause to listen, but nothing breaks the deep silence.

You walk for what seems like hours. At first you think your eyes are playing tricks on you, but soon your fears are confirmed: The flashlight is getting weaker. A short while later it goes out completely, and you are left in utter darkness.

You and Simone hold hands so as not to lose each other as you make your way through the tunnel. Suddenly you run into a wall. You can tell by feeling around that there is a passage to your left and one to your right. Who knows where either one leads?

If you go to your left, turn to page 104.

If you go to your right, turn to page 117.

Simone has recovered from her shock. "One thing is certain," she says coldly, "we can't risk setting Raoul free until we know what has happened to Marie and Jean-Paul. So either you stay here and guard him while I make some discreet inquiries, or we lock him up somewhere and go look for our friends together."

If you lock Raoul up, turn to page 10.

If you stay and guard him, turn to page 105.

132

You watch the tank crawl by. You'll wait for a smaller fish to fry.

A little while later a troop convoy passes, with truck after truck packed with soldiers. The sun rises higher in the sky. You have an uncomfortable feeling that all those men will soon be combing the valley for you.

Jean-Paul taps you on the shoulder and points down the valley. A search party is slowly coming toward you. Simone points to another search party closing in on you from the other direction.

"Let's get across the road," you whisper. The four of you bend low and run across. But troops are coming from the other side, too. Slowly and methodically they tighten the net around you. There is no escape.

The End

ABOUT THE AUTHOR

This is JAY LEIBOLD's first Choose Your Own Adventure book. His second, *Grand Canyon Odyssey,* will be published soon, and he is hard at work on a third, which is set during the American Revolution. He was born in Denver, Colorado, and now lives in San Francisco, California.

ABOUT THE ILLUSTRATOR

RALPH REESE is a contributing artist to the *National Lampoon.* His illustrations have appeared in *Scholastic* and the *Electric Company* magazines. He has also created comic strips and features for *Crazy* and *Epic.* His first children's book was called *The First Crazy Book,* written by Byron Preiss; in the Choose Your Own Adventure series he has illustrated *House of Danger, The Race Forever, Escape, Space Patrol,* and *Trouble on Planet Earth.* A former president of the Academy of Comic Book Art, Mr. Reese has won numerous awards for his art. He has, in addition, designed animated television commercials, worked in major advertising agencies, and taught illustration professionally.